BEING A BETTER BEAR

The Ethics of *Cheezee Pleazees*

By

Leslie E. Sekerka

With Illustrations by

William and John Jenkins

Atherton
Menlo Imprint
2019

Published by Menlo Imprint, Menlo College, 1000 El Camino Real, Atherton, CA USA 94027

This book is a work of fiction. Names, characters, places, and incidents are either a product of the author's imagination or are used fictitiously, and any resemblance to actual persons, living or dead, business establishments, events or locales is entirely coincidental.

Library of Congress Cataloging-in-Publication Control Number: 2019930168
Being a better bear, the ethics of cheezee pleazees/ by Leslie. E. Sekerka

1. Children's Literature 2. Ethical Responsibility 3. Moral Development

Print ISBN 13: 978-0-9915196-6-8

10 9 8 7 6 5 4 3 2 1 15 16 17 18 19
Printed in the United States of America First Edition, June 2019

On acid-free paper
Book design by Fred's team

Menlo Imprint, Menlo College
Ethics in Action Center
http://www.childrensethics.com/

For our dear brother John
and all of the other little bear cubs
out there reading in the forest.

BEING A BETTER BEAR

Fred Bear is a good bear (more or less). He likes to think he will do the right thing. But sometimes he has to pause, lean on his paw, and ask himself:

Fred learned about being ethical when he was just a young cub.

He knew that being a better bear was about exercising his moral muscles. This meant looking for ways to be helpful and remembering to finish his chores and homework before going out to play.

Sometimes it was hard to be ethical. But Fred learned that by doing the right thing, he felt better about himself and could sleep soundly at night.

Not too long ago, Fred's desire to be a better bear was put to a test. A temptation got the better of him and he forgot about wanting to be ethical. Here's the story of how that happened.

When the Bear School bell rang at noon, the hungry cubs knew it was time for lunch. The young bears raced to gather round. Gleefully, they traded and shared their goodies. It was always great fun!

After the cubs finished eating, they loved to have a grape tossing contest. They competed to see who could catch the most before the bell rang for class.

Fred noticed his buddy Seymour was eating something unusual. They were bright orange crackers that he had never seen or tried before.

Looking at the package, Fred exclaimed, "How cool!"

Seymour responded, "They're called *Cheezee Pleazees.*"

Fred said, "What a funny name!" Then he burst out laughing, "Oh, ha ha ha ha! That's hilarious!"

Seymour poured some of the goodies into his friend's paw. After trying them, Fred announced that the treats were a fabulous taste sensation.

After just one bite, Fred imagined that he was floating on a fluffy orange cloud of *Cheezee Pleazees.*

He smiled and melodically sang out loud, "Ahhhhhh...most delicious!!!"

Fred decided that this was his new favorite food. The cheese tasting bobbles were the best, tastiest, and most delightful treats in the entire world! Fred even thought they were fun to say. So he cheered over and over again, "*Cheezee Pleazees, Cheezee Pleazees, Cheezee Pleazees, Cheezee Pleazees!*"

Although he didn't realize it at the time, Fred became so consumed by his desire to get more of the delicious treats that he forgot about his desire to be a better bear.

Fred knew that being ethical meant working hard to do the right thing, to think about others more than yourself, and to do more than what you have to do. But those healthy thoughts went out of his head, as he envisioned tossing the orange treats into his mouth,

one

after

the

other.

Upon arriving home from school that afternoon, he announced to his mother, "All I ever want for breakfast, lunch, and dinner are *Cheezee Pleazees*!"

She responded, "My dear little cub, to be a healthy bear you need to eat your fish, fruits, grains, and vegetables. As much as you would like to have treats for every meal, that would not be healthy."

"And besides," she added, "Some snacks are made with unnatural ingredients that are simply not good for you. They aren't even real food! I'm sorry honey, but I'm not buying them."

This made Fred quite upset. "How could this be?" he thought to himself. *Cheezee Pleazees* were the perfect food! All he could think about were those bite-sized cheesy morsels and this wonderful new taste sensation that made him want more,

and more,

and more,

and more,

and more!

"But ***Mooooooooom***!!! I have to have them," he declared. Fred was about to cry, he was so angry and upset. "This just isn't fair! Why does Seymour get to have *Cheezee Pleazees*, but not me? Who cares about fruits and vegetables anyway? *Grrrrr*," he snarled.

Plotting to get more *Cheezee Pleazees*, Fred went upstairs to his room to make plans. After all, his mother hadn't said "no." She just said that she wouldn't buy them. "*Hmmmm.* I wonder how I can get some by myself," he pondered.

Unfortunately, this decision was not a wise one. The distraction to get his paws on more *Cheezee Pleazees* had become so over-whelming that Fred was no longer thinking about being his best self. *Cheezee Pleazees* had, in fact, become an ethical issue for the young cub.

In the past, Fred always made a habit of trying to be a better bear each and every day. For example, he would help by drying the dishes, sorting the garbage, sweeping the kitchen floor, putting his toys away, and brushing his teeth before going to bed.

Indeed, Fred truly took pride in being a better bear, which meant being ethical throughout each and every day. But with *Cheezee Pleazees* now racing through all of his thoughts, he was thinking less about being ethical and MORE about how to get his paws on *Cheezee Pleazees*. Fred usually loved to play Red Rover with his friends. But now he was much too distracted to enjoy the activity.

When his math teacher asked him to subtract 2 from 3, he couldn't answer because he hadn't been paying attention. Fred was far too busy thinking about how he could get more *Cheezee Pleazees*.

Mr. Specs, the geography teacher, was astonished that Fred wasn't paying attention to his lesson about the world. Fred was daydreaming, thinking about...well...YOU KNOW WHAT!

In art class Fred's drawing looked like a plate filled with *Cheezee Pleazees*!

When the school bell rang, an idea came to Fred in a flash. "Ah ha! I know! I'll ask Seymour if he will sell me some of his. I can use my milk money!"

When Seymour heard the idea, he grinned. He said, "Sure, Freddy. I'll trade you my CPs for your milk money whenever you want. Not a problem."

The cubs both said, "DEAL!" and shook paws on it.

Fred was off and running with his treats.

As the days passed and this arrangement continued, Fred wasn't feeling very good inside. In fact, he was upset and worried. But he couldn't figure out why.

Each morning his mother would say, "Don't forget your milk money, my dear!" Then each night, it was getting harder and harder to talk to her.

Fred was feeling guilty and ashamed of himself for being dishonest with his mom. He was living a lie. He had been given money for milk and instead of doing what his mother entrusted him to do, he was spending it on his own selfish desires. Without realizing it, a source of pleasure had become a source of distress.

One night at dinner, Fred's anxiety was showing. His mother said, "My dear cubby, you haven't talked about your friends lately. How is Seymour? What's new at school?"

Fred burst out, "I don't know! I don't care about him or school anymore. And who wants to drink milk anyhow?!"

Surprised by Fred's outburst and the lack of manners, his mother asked him to excuse himself from the table. She suggested that it might be a good idea to take a time out.

Fred had come to understand that time outs weren't all that bad. He learned that they gavc him a break, a moment where he could calm down. In that space, he could think about why he was upset and why the situation wasn't going so well.

Fred started by thinking about getting a great big plate of *Cheezee Pleazees*. But that didn't help at all. So Fred decided to go to his room and relax.

"Hmmmm, what's wrong here?" he wondered. "Why am I so upset?"

Playing with his favorite green truck, reading, and just listening to the birds seemed to help a little.

Although these activities calmed him down, they did not resolve the problem.

Just then, his mother knocked at the door. Fred was glad to see her. He said, "Sorry, Mama. I wasn't mad at you. I'm unhappy because things aren't going so good right now."

She asked, "Is it because of those *Cheezee Pleazees*?"

Quickly, Fred responded, "What *Cheezee Pleazees*?"

"Oh, the ones you have been buying at school every day," she said calmly.

"Hey, how did you know about that?" Fred cried out.

“We mothers have our ways of knowing,” she said with a little smile (as she pictured Fred’s orange paw prints everywhere).

Puzzled by his mother’s amazing bear wisdom, he decided he might as well tell her the whole story. He knew he had done wrong. But at the time, it felt like he couldn’t help himself.

"Fredrick, you must learn how to manage your desires. Sometimes we want things that are just not good for us. We have to practice controlling ourselves, showing restraint, and exercising the moral muscle of self-regulation. Your cravings for these treats caused you to forget all about being a better bear," she explained.

"You mean being dishonest with my milk money?" asked the young cub.

"That's exactly right!" his mother affirmed. "If you have trouble doing the right thing, maybe it's because you are overwhelmed by a temptation."

“When you experience that sort of thing, it’s time to take a step back, pause, reflect, and pay attention to your emotions,” his mother explained. Comforting Fred, she added, “It is important to get some help.”

But Fred was still confused about why the treats became an ethical issue for him but not for his friends.

His mother explained, “Everyone is different. We all have certain cravings that can distract us from being better bears. It is important to pay attention, recognize, and manage what tempts us.”

Fred realized that although his friends liked *Cheezee Pleazees*, the desire to have more of them did not interfere with their ability to play, pay attention in school, and be ethical.

Even though the treats had caused him a lot of trouble, the thought of never having them again made him feel sad.

Seeing his disappointment, his mother said, “I have an idea! Let’s make our own! They will be a bit different. But I promise you they will be better than the ones you have been buying!”

Fred jumped up and followed his mother to the kitchen. It seemed almost magical that you could make treats in your own home.

Fred sat on the big stool and helped with stirring. They put scoops of the dough onto a cookie tray. Once in the oven, they watched the little mounds grow.

The smells coming from the kitchen were delicious, and the waiting was almost unbearable! Fred's mother said this was practice at being patient.

Finally, out they came, all puffed up and golden brown.

"Hey Mom," asked Fred, "Why aren't they orange?"

"It's because they are homemade, using only natural ingredients," she explained. "And, they are made with love, which has no color," his mother added.

Finally the fresh snacks were cool, and it was time for the big taste test.

"Let's see how you like them Freddy," his mother said, as she presented him with a plate of the freshly baked treats.

Fred exclaimed, "These are tremendous, Mama! I know. Let's call them, *Freddy Delights*!"

His mother smiled and nodded eagerly in agreement.

"Why that's perfect, my dear. And there's plenty to go around. So let's make up a basket for your class, so you can share them with everyone."

Fred realized that the most important moral muscle of all is self-regulation. This means you have to recognize and control selfish urges and remember that what you value more than treats is to be a better bear. It is important to pay attention to temptation if you want to maintain your moral strength. By staying ethically fit, you can experience a lifetime of shared joy.

Now you can be a better bear too!

Fred invites you to continue the story.

Using your crayons put yourself into the picture.

HOME SWEET
HOME

THE END

Special Thanks

We thank Lucy Sekerka, Erin O'Donnell, the Menlo College library staff and students, along with all of Fred's family and friends who generously shared their time and talent.

Fred is especially grateful to the James Hervey Johnson Charitable Educational Trust, as they helped to make this book series possible.

Thank you!